INDIAN MOUND FARM

INDIAN

MOUND FARM

Elizabeth Coatsworth

Drawings by FERMIN ROCKER

THE MACMILLAN COMPANY
Collier-Macmillan Ltd., London

For Henry, with whom I first
saw Indian Mound Farm

The Macmillan Company
Collier-Macmillan Canada, Ltd., Toronto, Ontario

Library of Congress catalog card number: 69-18234

Printed in the United States of America
FIRST PRINTING

Contents

Pamelia

Pamelia
Acted like a flower,
Pamelia
Was a flower
Growing in the grass.

Sometimes
She was careless,
Sometimes
She was naughty,
But everyone loved
To see Pamelia pass.

Pamelia
Was a flower,
People smiled
To see her,
Pretty as a flower,
Simple as one, too.

Pamelia
Was a flower
Growing
In the sunlight,
It was her heart that told her
Always what to do.

INDIAN MOUND FARM

I   THE GYPSIES

There was the jingle of a doorbell through the house. Everyone else was busy, and Pamelia ran down the stairs, breathlessly, and threw open the door, while the other three Stowe children appeared on the landing to watch. Outside a misty rain was falling, a cool, early June rain veiling with a silver light the green of the lawns and trees.

Sheltered by the veranda, two women stood, an old woman and a young woman, wearing shawls and wide skirts. Their shoes were muddied and wet, and raindrops hung in the girl's braids, but she held her head so boldly that they looked like ornaments.

"Good morning, pretty miss," the old woman said in a playful, singsong voice. "Would your mamma like to buy any nice willow baskets today, to help the poor gypsies?"

Louise, who was thirteen, more than three years older than Pamelia, called from the stair, "I'll ask Mamma," and Pamelia and the gypsies stood waiting. Pamelia could hear the little tap-tapping of the small raindrops and the deeper, slower tapping of the big drops that gathered and fell from the tips of the leaves, and the laughing gurgle of the water from the spouts. The gypsies stood at ease, their bright dark eyes seeing everything in the hall, noticing the handsome rug, the polished rail of the stair, and the mirror in the carved hatrack by the door. They rearranged the baskets in their hands until the best ones were ready to show, and waited with the look of birds about to burst into song.

A cart, with an ambling horse between its shafts and another horse tied at the tailboard, drove up to the curb and waited, too. There was a stovepipe sticking from one side of the cart, with a wisp of smoke drifting from it into the rain, and a dirty little boy peered from the driver's seat, where he sat between a man and a dog.

"They live in it," thought Pamelia. "Oh, how I wish I might go with them!"

In all her nearly ten years, she had never been away from home, had never seen any town but Cincinnati, had never been out of the sound of the voices of her brother and sisters. Perhaps standing there in the open door, silent, watching the gypsies, was as near to adventure as Pamelia had yet come.

"Mamma says she is sorry, but she can't use any baskets," came Louise's voice behind her.

The thing like a song that had waited with the gypsy

women was gone. Their eyelids lowered over their bright eyes, their silence took on a different quality, their thin shoulders shrugged under their bright, damp shawls.

Without a word, they turned to go.

Pamelia couldn't bear it. "I have twenty-five cents of my own," she cried. "Have you any twenty-five-cent baskets?"

"Pamelia!" breathed Louise, horrified once more by her sister's impulsiveness. With Pamelia everyone was either saying, "Wake up, Pamelia," when she was lost in a daydream, or "Come back, Pamelia," when she *did* wake up.

The older woman went on down the steps as though she hadn't heard, but the girl turned back.

"I have a pretty little basket for you, my gay miss," she said. "Here it is, with my love, and I will take your twenty-five cents, since that is all you have."

"Wait a moment," Pamelia begged. "I must get the money out of my handkerchief case."

She raced upstairs, tore open the heavy drawer of the walnut bureau in the room she shared with Louise, and found the silk and cardboard case in which her handkerchiefs lay neatly folded. There, at the bottom, was the twenty-five cent piece and, thank goodness, a ten-cent piece, too, that she had forgotten. She raced down the stairs again, her face rosy with running.

The gypsy girl was still waiting, while Louise watched

her rather suspiciously from the shelter of the door.

"Here!" cried Pamelia. "I have more than I thought!"
And she thrust her money into the gypsy's brown hand.

A mocking smile lighted the girl's face, but her eyes
were friendly, and she spoke in the playful, caressing
voice she had used from the first.

"Thank you, little heart," she said. "We shall soon
meet far from here."

"But I never go anywhere. I wish I did!" stammered

Pamelia, while Louise giggled, and the giggle was taken up by Tom, who was leaning over the bannister, and by little Sue on the landing.

The young woman tossed her hair, braided with ribbons, back from her brown cheeks.

"You will make a journey and we shall meet again," she said, and walked down the steps and up the street. The gypsy man chirruped to the horse and the cart followed along the curb.

Two weeks later Pamelia stood beside her favorite aunt at the rail of the *Prairie Belle,* headed for St. Louis and Aunt's farm, where Pamelia was to spend the summer. The whole thing had come to pass like one of her daydreams. She still couldn't understand how it had happened, how Aunt had come for a visit, and had invited Pamelia to go back with her, and Pappa and Mamma had consented and here she was.

Pamelia was a town girl and she had never imagined the size of America until she saw it from the decks of the *Prairie Belle*. Mile after mile stretched out before her eyes, wooded, flat, at most times apparently uninhabited. Sometimes on the vast river there was a smudge of smoke ahead, and then the passengers knew that they would meet another steamer. Sometimes the *Prairie Belle* stopped at a lonely woodyard to take on fuel, and sometimes she pulled in at a landing where the whole town was lined up to watch for her arrival.

Late on the second afternoon, as they breasted the hidden currents of the Mississippi, they again saw smoke ahead of them, but this time the *Prairie Belle* came no nearer to it.

"I wonder if we'll overtake it?" Pamelia exclaimed.

"Doesn't it seem to you that we're going faster?" Aunt asked.

Pamelia looked overhead. Certainly the smoke from the twin stacks was thicker and darker than it had been. The *Prairie Belle* seemed to tremble and the panting sound of her engines had increased, and the slap, slap, slap of the sternwheel came faster. All at once, the dangerous, swirling brown river, the low, scarcely varying shores had become a race track where the two rival vessels might compete before the eyes of everyone along the banks. St. Louis would furnish a grandstand finish.

Pamelia, who had been half lost in the dream of the flowing river, was roused by the excitement. She spent hours glued to the rail and could scarcely bear to go in for supper. Aunt, as often, felt the way Pamelia did. As night came on, the scene became wilder and wilder. The sky darkened and a waning moon rose out of the east. Ahead, they could see the lighted decks of the other steamer and the glow of her smoke, as she raced before them, stubbornly battling the onrush of the Mississippi.

"She's the Susy B. on the New Orleans to St. Louis run, and we'll get her!" the mate told Aunt as he passed by. "She's a good boat, but our pilot, Alf Lemming, is the best man on the river. He'll cut corners the Susy B. don't even know are there."

That night it was hard to go to bed, but at last Aunt felt that they really must, and they went unwillingly to their stateroom. After what seemed a long time Pamelia fell asleep and slept until Aunt woke her next morning. They dressed in a jiffy and hurried out on deck. It was broad daylight, and most of the passengers were already at the rail. Many of the men hadn't gone to bed at all. Pamelia could see that the *Susy B.* was nearer. An hour later she could even make out separate people on the decks.

The suspense was becoming almost unendurable. Ahead, they could see St. Louis and the spires of its churches. In the cabins the suitcases were still unpacked. In the galley the breakfast dishes were unwashed.

The *Prairie Belle* drew ahead, drew ahead. It was meeting the wash of the *Susy B.* In a moment now it would be drawing abreast of the other steamboat, but somehow the moment never came. The *Susy B.*'s stokers threw more fuel into her furnaces. Now the smoke was coming in great rolls from her twin stacks, her wheel was thrashing madly at the stern.

Close together the two vessels entered into the final stretch of the river. News of the race had spread and the waterfront was lined with people. The *Prairie Belle* put on her final burst of speed. Her bow drew up along her rival's side. Pamelia, without knowing it, was jumping up and down with excitement, Aunt was twisting a handkerchief between her fingers, and people around them, men and even ladies, were shouting, "Go it, Prairie Belle! Go it! Go it!"

And like a horse urged on, the *Prairie Belle* struggled forward. She was driving ahead, almost bow to bow with the *Susy B.,* and a burst of clapping and shouting came from her partisans on the shore, when a miracle happened. Using some last store of power, the *Susy B.* shook off her rival. Panting, shaking, belching out a pall of smoke, she drew ahead and turned in for her landing, uttering a whistle like a shriek of triumph, while a yell of applause greeted her from her friends on shore.

The *Prairie Belle* passed her, on her way to her own berth, with a hoot of defiance, and Alf Lemming leaned out of the pilothouse to call to the other pilot, "Best two out of three, Bill! We'll get you next run, sure."

But the *Prairie Belle* had been beaten, beaten before the eyes of half St. Louis. Pamelia should have been brokenhearted. She was surprised to find herself skipping as she hurried off after Aunt to help with their belated packing.

"Do you know, Aunt, I'm glad the Susy B. won?" she said, astonished.

Aunt stopped and looked at her, astonished, too. "Why?" she asked.

Pamelia wrinkled her brow under its smooth coppercolored bang. "I don't know exactly. Is it because it's so horrid to be overtaken, even when it's only Louise overtaking me? When anything's hunted, I always hope it will escape, and the Susy B. was like a hunted thing, wasn't she? I feel as if she had escaped, and I can't help being glad."

Aunt smiled a smile that was very like Pamelia's. "When I stop to think about it," she said, "I think that I'm glad, too."

The Travelers

Where does the rain come from?
Where have the clouds all been?
What rivers have they crossed?
What mountains have they seen?

The rain comes down like Niagara.
Was it part of those mighty falls?
In rush and roar and thunder
The great Pacific calls.

Did the Gulf of Mexico cradle it?
When the sun comes out, will the rain
Climb up the ladders of brightness
To be off on its travels again?

2   INDIAN MOUND FARM

Paddy-pad, paddy-pad, went the hoofs of Chief, the sorrel horse, along the old National Pike. Pamelia found it very cozy sitting between Uncle and Aunt in the buggy. It was a fine day and the buggy's top had been put down so that she might see everything for miles around. St. Louis lay behind them across the river. All about them stretched flat, black bottom land, once the bed of an even greater Mississippi. Everywhere the young corn was rising, bright green against the dark soil. The farms with their outbuildings seemed like broody hens with their chicks under their wings. As far as Pamelia's glance could go, there was no rise of land anywhere in all this one great cornfield.

At first she enjoyed this new world, but then she found herself thinking, "It's too flat. When the corn grows tall, it will smother us. I'm not at all sure that I like it here."

Perhaps Uncle noticed that Pamelia was very quiet and guessed she was thinking of home and feeling her first pangs of homesickness. "Can you drive?" he asked, and when she nodded, he gave her the reins.

"Chief is a good horse," he told her. "He's young and fast. Blowing paper is about the only thing he's afraid of."

Driving a new horse took most of Pamelia's attention. She never noticed the change in the landscape until Aunt exclaimed, "Here we are! That's Indian Mound Farm ahead." Then Pamelia looked up quickly and, wonder upon wonders, there close ahead rose a whole group of hills and hillocks, appearing straight out of the black cornland. The hill to the north of the pike was much the largest and highest. It had steep sides and a flat top, with a wide terrace halfway up. On its top stood a red farmhouse from whose kitchen chimney the smoke was blowing cheerfully, and there were barns and sheds on the lower terrace. A road wound up its side.

Uncle took back the reins and pulled in Chief before starting up the steep drive. "How do you like Indian Mound Farm?" he asked. "You've never lived on an Indian mound before, now, have you?"

Pamelia's eyes opened wider and wider. "An Indian mound?" she repeated. "Is this a real Indian mound? I thought it was just a name you liked."

"Indeed, it's a real mound! Made by the Mound Builders," Aunt exclaimed. "Haven't you ever been to the famous one near Cincinnati, shaped like a serpent with an egg in its mouth? But then lots of people aren't as interested in Indian mounds as we are, perhaps because we live on one. Do you see the schoolhouse across

the road? It has a mound of its own, not as high nor large as ours, of course. The farm's mound is ninety-nine feet high. But the schoolhouse mound is steeper. When school is open, you ought to see the children come flying down the path at the closing bell! I'm always afraid they'll break their necks."

Chief turned his face with its long, uneven, white blaze toward his driver, as though to say that he had rested enough, but Uncle gave Pamelia a moment more to look around her.

"They say it would have taken a thousand Indians at least five years to carry all the earth for it," Uncle added. "People think they must have had a temple on the top, where the farmhouse stands now."

Pamelia nodded. This was wonderful. A temple! And she was sure she understood why the mounds had been built. The Mound Builders, too, had thought the Mississippi bottom lands were too flat. Thank goodness, she wasn't going to live stifled by cornfields after all. She would be on a high hill, on the very spot where a temple had stood long, long ago.

Uncle whistled to Chief and raised the reins. Now they were off and climbing fast up the winding road, past the barns on the first terrace level, and up again, more steeply this time, to the flat cap of the pyramid, where they drew up with a flourish at the farm door.

While Aunt and Pamelia were getting out, an old man came up, wearing clothes too big for him and a battered hat, and took Chief's bridle to lead him to the stable. At first glance Pamelia thought, "He's a gypsy!" but then she saw that he must be something else, with another kind of mystery and power.

"That's Pawnee Sam," Uncle said as the old man led Chief away.

"Is he a Mound Builder?" Pamelia asked excitedly.

"Oh, no," said Uncle with a laugh, "but for all we know he *may* be descended from the Mound Builders."

Just then a pleasant, middle-aged woman appeared on the white steps to welcome them, and a dozen geese came waddling out from the grasses beside the drive.

Aunt introduced Pamelia to Mrs. Lewis, the house-keeper, and then to the geese.

"We don't keep a watchdog, Pamelia," she explained, "but these geese are better than any watchdog for driving off strangers. And, of course, I pluck them every year for feather beds. They won't bother you now that they've seen you with us."

Pamelia looked at the geese a little doubtfully. Pompey and Caesar and Mark Antony and Cleopatra and the rest seemed to be rather severe, with their long white necks like snakes, and their hard yellow beaks. They stood about in a semicircle, eyeing her, as it seemed, coldly, and apparently discussing her in low tones.

But away from the others stood a solitary goose. His feathers were not so spotless as theirs, his beak was not so bright a yellow, and the look he bent on Pamelia was hopeful and rather sad.

"Aunt, Aunt," called Pamelia as Aunt turned to go, "what's the name of that one over there, the sad one?"

Aunt stopped to look.

"Oh, that's poor Livy," she explained. "A sow stepped on his foot when he was a gosling and he's lame. Come in, dear. I'll show you your room."

There were six grown-up people at the farm—Uncle and Aunt, Mrs. Lewis, and the farm hands, Bill and Al and Pawnee Sam, the old Indian. They were all busy most of the day; and Pamelia, too, had her own chores,

though when they were finished she was free to do what she chose. For a few days she was very homesick and missed her own family, but after all there *was* something nice about being the only child on the place, so long as she knew she'd be going home in time for school. Everyone made a good deal of her, and no one said, "Wake up, Pamelia!" if she started daydreaming about the Mound Builders and their temple, and no one called, "Come back, Pamelia," if an idea came to her suddenly about something she wanted to see or do. She became more and more happy at the farm. Best of all she loved the evenings, when in the warm dusk the whole household had leisure to meet together, the women sitting in rocking chairs on the wide veranda, while the men lounged on the steps. Pamelia had a little white rocking chair of her own which had been Aunt's when she was Pamelia's age. Al brought an accordion, battered and mended, but still able to wheeze out its tunes gaily enough. As they sat watching the lights of St. Louis appear like fireflies across the river, Al would play a jig, or Bill, who had been a river-man, would sing an old song, or perhaps Uncle would tell a story. Only Pawnee Sam took no part in the singing or talking. Sometimes Pamelia tried to say something to him, but he scarcely answered. He was almost like a dark, wrinkled old ghost, the ghost of a Mound Builder, Pamelia thought. But in her imagination he looked very different. She saw him in charge of the mound building, watching the younger Indians bringing earth in their great baskets. Sam would say something encouraging to each as he went by and maybe reach out to balance a basket more securely on his head. *If* they carried the earth on their heads.

Perhaps they were like the later Indians and carried loads on their backs, supported by a thong across their foreheads. That's what Uncle thought was likely. No one knew. They did know that the Mound Builders wore necklaces of fresh-water pearls from the Mississippi and had ornaments of shining mica fastened on their deerskin clothing. Deep in the earth, people had found these ornaments, shaped like thunderbirds or snakes or arrows. Uncle said such fine things must have been worn on feast days. But Pamelia, in her mind's eye, saw her imaginary Pawnee Sam always dressed in his best, very different from the old clothes he wore today.

With Only Your Iron Pride

How easy it is to be proud
When you have everything:
Youth and good looks and money
With which to buy what you want.
How easy it is to be proud
When people turn as you pass;
Perhaps you have fame as well,
And everyone knows your name.

How hard it is to be proud
When you are old and have nothing,
When your race has died out or departed
And you take orders or starve.
How hard it is to be proud
Without possessions or power,
With only the will to endure,
With only your iron pride.

3   THE STORM

Like water pouring out of the pitcher when Pamelia filled the glasses for supper, the hours passed. How were Pappa and Mamma? What had Louise been doing? And had Tom built the tree house he was talking about when she left? Did Sue still tag after him wherever he went? But already the old life in Cincinnati, which had seemed to Pamelia the whole world, was growing a little unreal.

One morning toward the beginning of her visit, Pamelia stood on the porch steps looking about her. From the top of the Indian mound on which the farmhouse stood, she could see for miles over the flat cornfields toward the distant smoke and spires of St. Louis. Here and there another farm, with its trees and barns, rose like an island from the corn, and nearer at hand there were mounds, some basket-shaped and some square with very steep sides. On one of them stood the schoolhouse, with a path scrambling up to its twin doors. While she was looking at it, Aunt's flock of watchdog geese came waddling about her feet, staring at her severely from their pale eyes, and demanding food.

Any companionship was something, and Pamelia ran to the kitchen for cracked corn and dry bread, but though the geese ate what she brought greedily, they seemed as disagreeable and disapproving as ever.

"Hiss and whisper all you want!" Pamelia exclaimed, shaking the crumbs from her apron. "I don't like you any better than you like me, and I think your eggs taste nasty!"

The geese looked at her down their beaks, holding their absurd heads high, and then waddled off, still talking to one another. Only lame Livy lingered behind the flock. Food was harder for Livy to catch than for the others. He was less proud than they, more willing to pick up the very little crumbs that the rest of the flock thought not worth stooping for.

Pamelia watched him for a while.

"I believe you're rather nice," she said at last. "There's a cooky in my pocket. I was going to eat it myself, but you shall have half of it."

She sat down on the lowest step and Livy came close to her. He was willing to take the pieces of cooky from her fingers, and she noticed that he did not grab at them greedily like the other geese. He looked at her sadly when he had eaten his half and waited. Pamelia gave him her half of the cooky, too.

Soon she was feeding Livy off and on all day. She taught him tricks, and he would hunt in her pockets for tidbits. When she weeded the fenced-in garden back of the house, or picked beans, or pulled radishes for Aunt, Livy would limp after her as far as he could come, and then wait for her at the fence gate, honking companionably.

When Pamelia began to explore farther afield, Livy followed. If she ran, he would waddle hastily after her, honking as if to beg her to wait for him. He was something of a nuisance, but he was company, too. When she felt lonely for the other children, Pamelia even took him as far as the schoolhouse, whose key hung on a nail behind the farmhouse door.

"The school's on our land," Aunt explained. "During vacation I always walk over there once in a while, to make sure that everything is all right. I don't see why you shouldn't go there if you like, Pamelia. But be sure to remember to bring back the key and to leave everything at the schoolhouse as you find it."

After that, the schoolhouse became Pamelia's own Indian temple, and she loved it dearly. More and more often she would make her way to where it stood on its high pyramid of a hill. If there had been a big temple where the farm stood, there must have been a little temple here, and now the temple-schoolhouse was hers, and hers alone for this summer, and perhaps other summers, too, because Aunt and Uncle had invited her to come back next year. Pamelia saw the schoolroom just as it was: teacher's desk, blackboards and all, and yet at the same time she saw it as a mysterious place with an altar where the desk stood. On this altar nothing had ever been offered but the first strawberries, blueberries, shells, feathers, pearls, and corn. The Indian children, Pamelia thought, had loved this temple. Perhaps it had been theirs, as the present schoolhouse was now hers. During these few weeks Pamelia inherited it all for her very own. Even if it had never been a temple, she would have loved the place. Its windows had a wide view that gave her the sense of being in a nest in a treetop. While Livy waited in the shade outside, Pamelia amused herself drawing pictures on the blackboard, or glancing into old schoolbooks standing on the shelf back of the teacher's desk. It was at this desk that she wrote letters home, or sometimes just sat, her chin on her hands, and dreamed, with wide, unseeing eyes.

One day in early August it was even hotter than usual. Pamelia sewed with Aunt on the veranda, but about the middle of the afternoon she grew restless. Along the horizon clouds were gathering for a thunderstorm, the leaves rustled drily, and the air felt tense with change. Pamelia knew she couldn't sit still much longer.

"Please, Aunt," she begged, "may I go over to the schoolhouse with Livy? I'll be back soon."

Aunt threaded a needle and looked at the sky. "It's going to storm," she said. "Why don't we make some lemonade instead?"

Pamelia looked so disappointed that Aunt smiled.

"Go if you like, dear," she agreed, "but don't be gone

long. It won't rain for a couple of hours, I should think, but when it rains, it will rain hard. Are you sure you wouldn't like to make lemonade?"

But what Pamelia really wanted was to take the pins and needles out of her legs, and Aunt nodded agreement.

Off went Pamelia and Livy. They passed Al near the barns and had a distant glimpse of Uncle mending the fence of the pasture where the hogs had broken through. Dust lay thick on all the weeds along the road, and a passing wagon dripped dust from its revolving wheels.

The heat in the corn was almost unendurable. Now and then a low rumbling came from the sky. Livy limped and went even more slowly than usual. Pamelia had to boost him up the steepest parts of the school-house path.

She took the key from her pocket, and, once inside, flung open the windows to let in what air there was.

The sky grumbled, was silent, grumbled again. A queer blue-black color, like ink, spread itself along the horizon, sopped up by the wadded clouds. Pamelia felt more restless than ever. Perhaps after the long drought the Mound Builder priests were praying for rain and now all the tribe—and Pamelia with them—were waiting to see if the rain would come.

The thunder came nearer. The sun shone very brightly on the clouds, and the great cornfields stretched green against the sunlit blackness. Everything was touched by a momentary beauty. Pamelia knew it was time to go. Rather doubtfully she left the shelter of the schoolhouse to join Livy. As they stood at the top of the path, the clouds overtook the fleeing sun, and almost immediately a flicker of lightning and a crash showed that the storm had begun, though still the rain held off.

Pamelia ran back into the schoolhouse to shut the windows. Then she locked the door and hurried down the path with Livy following more slowly, limping.

"Hurry, Livy!" Pamelia called, making her way into the thick-growing corn. "I'll be glad when we're out on the pike and in the open again," she thought.

For once, it seemed no time before the road lay before her. For a moment she stood still, looking at the vast, uneasy sky.

"The clouds are great travelers," she thought. "Much greater travelers even than the people who go by here on their way to the West. Greater travelers even than my gypsies."

Again lightning came lashing out of the clouds, sharp and crackling.

"The storm people are whipping up their horses," Pamelia thought. "They're in a hurry today."

A drop of rain fell smack on top of her head and another on her hand. The dusty road began to look freckled. Now that the rain had actually begun, she no longer felt in such a hurry to get home.

Followed by Livy, she began to dawdle. "I hope I get wet through," she thought. "It feels so cool. It's like walking along the bottom of the Mississippi."

Suddenly she saw something in the road in front of her. It was a dead toad, run over by some wagon. It looked sad, flattened out that way. Pamelia was always sorry for dead toads on the road, but Livy was not sorry for them at all and wanted to gobble them up.

"No, you don't," said Pamelia, shooing him away. "Livy, you let it alone. I'm going to bury it and you can be mourner."

Being mourner was not Livy's choice, but he stood back as he was told, and watched Pamelia dig a hole in the earth, put the toad into it, and cover it over. While she went to look for a headstone, Livy scouted around the grave, grumbling, but Pamelia chased him off again. In that black river soil there were only two stones in sight, one roundish and red, the other a gray oblong about the right size. Keeping one eye on Livy, Pamelia put the oblong stone upright at the head of the toad's grave, stood for a moment staring down at it, fending off Livy with a bare foot, and went on again, driving Livy before her to keep him away from the newly turned earth.

By this time it was raining hard. Pamelia could feel the drops running down her neck, pleasantly cool. Where had all this water come from that was pouring over her and over all the wide fields of corn? It came from the

gift-giving Mississippi and the Ohio certainly, those great rivers, and perhaps from the Gulf of Mexico. It had washed the sides of giant tortoises and sharks. Maybe the Great Lakes were in it. It felt like Niagara Falls, it felt like the breaking waves of the Pacific. These pelting, pouring, lightning-silvered drops of water might once have been spray along the beaches of South Sea islands.

By the time Pamelia and Livy had reached the farm they were both drenched. They looked half drowned, especially Pamelia, and Aunt made her drink a hot glass of peppermint tea.

"I should never have let you go out with a storm coming," said Aunt. "If you catch cold, I shall blame myself."

But Pamelia shook her head. "Oh, no! No!" she said. "It was a wonderful storm."

The River

Our land is like a leaf,
And its veins are the living rivers
With the Mississippi itself
As the long, strong central vein.
It takes from the land and gives,
The fields are rich with its bounty,
The corn grows high in black soil
Where the dark river has lain.

It has the smoke of its fogs
Like the smoke of Indian fires,
It can destroy or can save,
It is a savage still.
Old and wily and ruthless,
Who can forget the river?
Is there a man so bold
As to think he can break its will?

4   THE GYPSIES RETURN

Pamelia was sitting in her little white rocking chair beside her aunt, looking over a great basket of blackberries, nipping off stems and throwing away the squashed ones. The basket was set on a chair out of Livy's reach, and the good berries went into a dish pan, but the rejected ones fell, by fours or fives, into an old lard pail on the floor and this belonged to Livy. He half sat beside it, reaching in his pale yellow bill, every time so much as one berry fell. As usual he had stayed near the house when the rest of the flock waddled off to the creek in the meadow below the farmhouse.

"Sometimes there can't be enough for him even to taste," remarked Pamelia, her fingers flying.

"He seems happy," said her aunt.

After another companionable pause Aunt added, "That basket's coming to pieces. We need a new one."

Just as if genii had been summoned, there rose from the road below them the sound of far-off jangling, and mingled voices and hoof beats, slowly growing louder as they came nearer.

"Good!" exclaimed Aunt. "I've been hoping the gypsies would be coming soon. This is just about their time. Carry the blackberries into the kitchen, Pamelia, and ask Mrs. Lewis to lock the doors. There's no use taking chances."

At Pamelia's entrance, Mrs. Lewis looked up from the stove where she was baking.

"The gypsies!" she said. "I've got half a dozen leaky pots and pans I've been saving for them. I'll just lock up and bring them out."

They were all three with Livy on the veranda when the cart drove up. It was Pamelia's cart and exactly as she remembered it, except that now on the front seat sat the two women, with the boy between them, bright as dusty flowers, and the girl was driving the old horse, while pots and pans, hung on the cart, clanged and clanked. Between the hind wheels ran the dog, tongue out, but apparently paying little attention to the dust. Last rode the older man on the spare horse, and beside him came a stranger, a younger man glancing about like a hunter looking for game.

"Oh, Aunt," cried Pamelia. "Here come my gypsies!"

Mrs. Lewis picked up the pan and carried it into the kitchen.

"They're our gypsies, too," Aunt said. "They come every year," and she walked down the steps to greet

them, with Pamelia nodding and smiling at her side. She even nodded to the stranger, who gave her a brief hawk's smile. But her eyes were all for the gypsy girl who had jumped down from the high wagon seat and was already leading the old horse into the shade of the house, and bringing out his nose bag from somewhere in the crowded depths of the cart, superintended by an angry Livy.

"You have work for my father to do," she said to Pamelia's aunt in that caressing, faintly derisive voice which Pamelia remembered so well. "I see the pots and pans waiting. And my mother and I have brought baskets, prettier and cheaper than ever before."

"And I hope they're stronger, too," said Aunt goodnaturedly. "The last ones began to wear out after a few months."

The girl laughed, throwing back her head.

"You must have carried stones in them," she said. "Our baskets are strong, strong as well as beautiful! Like the one I gave you," she added, suddenly turning for the first time to Pamelia.

Pamelia was taken by surprise at the sudden attention. "Yes," she stammered. "It was very pretty, but I didn't have time to carry anything in it. I came here soon after you said I would take a journey."

"Oh, yes," said the gypsy. "I told you we should meet. And here we are."

The men had been busy setting up the equipment for soldering and were already at work on the tinware. The older man worked steadily and the younger man helped him, but not as if he were much interested. His eyes glanced here and there, settling now and again on Livy,

who was still hissing at the gypsy dog, lying motionless
under the wagon.

But the girl, although busy with bringing out baskets
and arranging them along the steps, was aware of what
was going on.

"No!" she suddenly exclaimed in a harsh, command-
ing voice, "No, Ambrose!"

"No, what?" he mocked her. "What have I done?"
She frowned.

"I know your thoughts," she said. "They are always
bad," and then she added in a low voice to Pamelia, "Is
that a tame goose? Shut him up in the kitchen while
we are here, if you want to see him again."

Ambrose laughed as Pamelia coaxed Livy into the
house. "Too old to be fit for the pot," he jeered. "How
suspicious girls are, anyway."

Pamelia found herself disliking him as much as the
gypsy girl seemed to. She shooed Livy into the kitchen.

"Mrs. Lewis," she begged, "may I please put some
newspapers on the pantry floor and shut Livy up where
he'll be safe? There's a new gypsy with the others and
he keeps looking at Livy. My friend, you know, the girl
who once came to our house, told me to shut Livy up."

"Of course," said Mrs. Lewis at once. "We can't lose
Livy. He's like one of the family." And she helped lay
down the newspapers and shoo the unwilling goose
into the pantry and then took the heel of a stale loaf of

bread and crumbled it on the papers to give Livy something he could enjoy while he was a prisoner.

By the time Pamelia came out into the sunshine, a
couple of baskets had been sold and the rest put back
in the wagon, and both the gypsy women were sitting
on the steps, while the little boy watched the men at
work or wandered about the yard, picking up things
and throwing them down.

"Keep out of the garden!" called his sister as he sidled
toward the gate. "I have my eye on you."

The little boy went back to the men, and the gypsy
girl smiled at Pamelia.

A little later she called, "Ambrose, what were you
doing in the barn?"

"Nothing," the man called back, spreading out his hands to show that they were empty. "I like to look around." And he strolled off, whistling, to join the older man.

"Maybe," said the girl in a low voice to Pamelia. "I hope so. When we met him at a camping place a short while ago he wanted to come with us. He's no good. Still, my father doesn't like to tell him to leave. It would make bad blood. But Ambrose is restless and we move too slowly for his taste. Then, too, we deal honestly at the farms which give us trade every year. That is not to his taste, either. He will leave of his own accord, my father thinks, and that will be better for everyone."

All too soon for Pamelia, the men finished their tinkering, the work was paid for, and the wagon drove off, clanging and clanking as before, with the girl driving, while her mother and little brother sat beside her, and the dog ran between the wheels. The two men followed, the younger man sweeping Pamelia a mocking bow.

"Your old lame goose can come out now," he called. "He isn't worth riding back for."

But Pamelia paid no attention to him. She was watching the wagon as it drove away in a cloud of sun-shafted dust. Once the driver leaned out, and a braceleted arm waved and Pamelia waved back. Then to its own harsh music, the little cavalcade passed out of sight down the steep road to the flat cornlands.

Gypsy Song

Oh gypsies! Dark gypsies!
People rail at you and revile you,
But everyone envies you, too,
You who follow a different way.
You have your own laws and customs,
You have no wish for a hearthstone,
Wherever you go you are strangers
Who pause, but never will stay.

You travel from land to land
As a sudden whim may take you.
You meet one another with joy
And as suddenly friend parts from friend.
You migrate as wild geese fly,
But no one is sure where you came from,
And no one knows what you seek,
Or when your search will end.

5 PAWNEE SAM

After the gypsies had driven away, life at Indian Mound Farm went on much as before. Pamelia picked vegetables in the cool of the morning in the garden behind its picket fence, while Livy watched mournfully from outside. She helped Aunt make the beds and dried dishes for Mrs. Lewis. Sometimes she spent long hours daydreaming at the schoolhouse, or sometimes, on warm afternoons, she sat beside Aunt on the porch in her own little rocking chair making gifts to take home to the family.

"'Well begun is half done,'" said Aunt, who was hemming sheets, and with her help and advice Pamelia was astonished to find how much she could get done: an embroidered runner for Mamma's bureau, a frilled apron for Louise, and six bean bags in different colors for little Sue.

Presents for Pappa and Tom were more difficult to decide upon, but Aunt was full of good ideas and Pamelia knitted Pappa red slippers to wear on winter nights in front of the fire, and for Tom she cut out and stuffed colored patterns of a cat and kitten, produced by Aunt from her storage chest.

"Of course Tom's too old to play with them," Pamelia said. "But he can keep them on his window seat. He'll like the way the pads of their paws show underneath."

The nice thing about all this present-making was that whenever Aunt saw that Pamelia was getting tired, or that her needle was growing sticky with the heat, or that her attention was wandering, she suggested that Pamelia had worked long enough, and that it was time for a glass of cold milk or of root beer, or wouldn't she like to go down to the stream with Livy or see what Pawnee Sam was doing? In fact Pamelia and Livy always liked to be with Sam. They made a curious trio, Pamelia in her

starched ruffles with new freckles across her nose, Pawnee Sam, short and dirty and silent, and Livy, limping and grasshopper-hunting at their heels. The old Indian paid no attention to the others, but he let them follow him at his work. Pamelia liked to listen to the songs he sang while he milked, although she didn't understand the words. Perhaps the Mound Builders had sung the same songs.

When one day she asked Pawnee Sam what they were about, he said, gruffly, "That one, song of spring and young man wondering this year he have enough ponies maybe get married to girl he knows."

Sam answered her questions but never as though he wanted to talk. Somehow he always held her off and Pamelia was sure that he would rather be alone. Of all the people on the farm, she most wanted Pawnee Sam for a friend. But however friendly she might be, he kept his usual wooden reserve. Sometimes she caught him glancing at her, but she could not read the expression of his eyes, like splinters of black glass under his drooping lids.

Pamelia tried again.

"Why do you sing to the cows?" she asked.

"More milk," Pawnee Sam answered briefly, turning away, and at last Pamelia, discouraged, went off to take the swill to the pigpen. The pigs were feeding in clover, but they still enjoyed sour milk or the scrapings from the dishes, and though Pamelia didn't like the smell of the pails, or the flies which followed her at feeding time, she did enjoy seeing the pigs scramble at her call.

"Pig! Pig! Pig!" she would shout, and the pigs would come nimbly running, their long ears shaking, their snouts twisting eagerly, their little eyes with their pale lashes full of greed and intelligence. Big pigs and little pigs, they came crowding together, climbing into the trough, grunting and pushing, gobble, gobble, gobble, and then coaxing for more.

In the evening she played checkers on the kitchen table with Uncle, or Al, the champion player at the farm. She offered to teach Pawnee Sam to play, but as usual he shook his head without answering. He got on well enough with the other men, but he kept to himself, most often working alone. In his old clothes and big stained hat, he was a rather pathetic figure, and yet he had dignity, too.

One evening Pamelia noticed that there was a new tear across the shoulder of his coat.

"Give me your coat, Pawnee Sam, and I'll mend it for you," she said, for in her large family both Louise and she helped her mother with the mending.

Sam looked at her for a long moment, and then without a word took off and handed her the coat. She found her sewing basket and mended it carefully, and after that he brought her his clothes when they were torn. He never thanked her, but she didn't mind. Surely, surely, someday he would begin to like her.

Aunt had a noticing eye.

"Pawnee Sam is peculiar, isn't he, Pamelia? I don't think he wants to be friends with anyone," she remarked one day. "Sometimes Uncle gets so provoked with his stand-offishness that he tells me he's going to fire him. But I tell Uncle *he*'d not be very friendly either if *his* people had once owned all this rich countryside and now *he* had to work for the new people who had taken over everything and left *him* with nothing. So Uncle nods to himself and says, 'He's a good worker,' and everything goes on as before for a while."

"Pawnee Sam's a good worker," Pamelia repeated, "and he's the descendant of the Mound Builders. He belongs here more than any of us do."

Aunt smiled as if once again she agreed.

All too soon it was almost time for Pamelia to leave Indian Mound Farm. A friend of Aunt's, a Mrs. Olmstead, was going from St. Louis to Cincinnati on the cars and she would take Pamelia with her. A train ride would be another exciting experience. Pamelia wondered if she would be able to breathe when traveling so fast, but "if other people can, I can," she told herself. Meantime she had to finish wrapping up the presents for her family. The day before she was to leave, she decided to explore all the farm for a last time for that summer. As usual she found Livy waiting and as usual he looked aggrieved until she brought out a thick slice of bread for him.

At that, Livy's eye brightened and when he had picked up the last crumb he followed her more cheerfully down to the second terrace where the barns stood. None of the men were around and even the horses were out, the team at work somewhere and Chief grazing. But Pamelia went in. She loved the shadowy place, with its hayloft and cobwebs, its stalls and harness room. Dreamily, she wandered about, peering into the mangers; watching the swallows fly in and out through the big doors; or lifting the heavy lid of the corn bin to run the kernels through her fingers. She only glanced into the harness room with its harnesses hanging on the wall, the carriage whip in the corner and the shelves crowded with liniments and bits of leather in need of mending.

On an earlier visit she had gone in and discovered the small shelf almost behind the door. On it, neatly arranged, were Mound Builder shells from the Gulf such as Uncle

had shown her, two or three arrowheads, and, in the place of honor at the center, what looked like the remnants of a tobacco pipe. Its red, stone stem was nearly whole and the bowl, which perhaps represented an animal, had deep nicks in it. Broken or not, the pipe had been cleaned and polished. Pamelia did not go in to look at it again, but she thought about it for a little while. What did it remind her of? She almost knew where she had seen something like that rounded red bowl, but then the knowledge faded.

Pamelia walked slowly back to the house with Livy tagging at her heels. The other geese arrived and Pamelia dutifully scattered corn for them, which they gobbled down, unpleasantly as ever.

"I wish you could see how you look, stooping and squabbling," she told them. "And Livy," she added crossly, "you look almost as bad as the others."

She thought of taking a pail of sour milk to the pigs, but somehow she didn't want to talk with them today. She wanted to get away from everyone, even from Aunt, whom she loved dearly. Only in the vegetable garden, weeding, would she be alone, and there she went, slowly working up and down the rows, while Livy waited unnoticed by the gate.

Next morning was fair and fine and the household was up early. The Olmsteads would stop for Pamelia in the early forenoon. It was a strange breakfast. Nobody felt like eating much, and Aunt and Pamelia scarcely ate at all.

"Don't bother with the dishes this morning, Pamelia. You have your traveling clothes on," said Mrs. Lewis. "Run along, and here's an old piece of cake for Livy."

Heavy-hearted, Pamelia wandered outdoors, passing by her suitcases waiting beside her special rocking chair on the porch. She saw Pawnee Sam weeding in the garden. Suddenly she remembered the broken pipe she had once seen in the harness room. There might be time to ask him about it before she had to leave.

She gave Livy his cake, and he limped after her to the picket gate and sat down philosophically for a dust bath, while she walked between two rows of tomato plants to speak to Sam.

He heard her coming but continued with his work.

"Sam," she said, "one day I was in the barn and I went into the harness room. There was a shelf there with some old shells and arrowheads on it. There was something else, too, a little like a pipe. What was that?"

"That was tobacco pipe of old-time Indians," Sam said, still going on with his work. "When old-time Indian smoked pipe, it meant peace. When he handed it to another Indian to smoke, it meant 'I am your friend.' Even if two tribes were at war they never fought

at the pipestone quarry, because the Great Spirit gave
that quarry to all tribes, not to just one." It was the first
time Pawnee Sam had really talked to her.

"How wonderful," thought Pamelia. She saw Pawnee
Sam with strings of Mississippi pearls about his neck
and mica thunderbirds fastened to his deerskin cloak, a
proud old man, lighting a peace pipe slowly, taking a
puff while the smoke rose in the air, and then passing
it to another Indian, who also took one puff and passed it
on to the next man in the circle of friends.

But Pawnee Sam had decided to say something more. A strong emotion had gripped him, and at last, after all these weeks, his tongue was loosened. Now he straightened up from his work and faced Pamelia, and she suddenly saw that his eyes were filled with anger and grief.

"I had a pipe, almost whole, only a couple of nicks, and just the end of the stem broken. Almost whole. The bowl was shaped like bear. The gypsy took it while I was working in lower field. I didn't find it was gone until next day. I thought I would follow him and kill him and take the pipe back. But then I thought, 'It is a peace pipe. There cannot be blood on a peace pipe,' so I did nothing. But my head is bowed."

"Oh, that horrible Ambrose!" cried Pamelia. "That's what he was up to in the barn that day!"

She looked at Pawnee Sam, with angry eyes. If only she could do something! Anything! Even say the right thing! But she felt helpless.

And as she stood there she saw Livy outside the fence, his long neck stretched out, his pale beak probing the grass.

And suddenly she remembered what the pipe bowl had reminded her of. Rain. The dead toad. And the two stones she had seen in the almost stoneless river-bottom soil when she was hunting for a headstone for the toad's

grave. She had taken the gray oblong one, but there had
been a round red one and Livy had reached for it and
pulled back, scolding. What foolishness! And yet, and
yet she must see.

"Aunt! Aunt!" she called to her aunt who had
appeared on the porch. "I'll be back in a minute!"

"But Mr. and Mrs. Olmstead will be here any time
now," her aunt called back. "You can't keep them
waiting."

"I'll run," cried Pamelia, already running in great
leaps down the road, with Livy limping far behind.

If her aunt called again after her, Pamelia did not
hear her. She flew across the barn terrace, and down
the second stretch of steep road and so reached the flats.
She knew just where to go and it wasn't far. But when
she got there, somehow everything seemed changed. She
went up and down along the road looking for the toad's
headstone. It should be standing up, but it wasn't. Far,
far off she could hear the sound of horses' hoofs. Mr. and
Mrs. Olmstead! She mustn't keep them waiting! She
had half turned to go back when she saw the oblong
stone, flat now, where perhaps a passing dog had knocked
it down. The red round stone had been about six feet
away, she thought.

Livy came bumbling up, honking at her reproach-
fully. She could hear the carriage wheels now, and felt

distracted. If only she had ten minutes to herself! She dropped desperately to her hands and knees, parting the weeds, feeling here and there. This was Livy's game. He, too, whispering to himself, began to hunt. Out of the corner of her eye, Pamelia saw that pale beak move downward, hesitate, and move on again. But she hurried forward to the spot Livy had reached toward, still on her knees, careless of what was happening to her go-away white stockings. And there it was, the rounded red stone!

The Olmsteads' carriage had almost reached the drive and was slowing down to rest the team as she began to dig into the dirt with her clean go-away hands, watched suspiciously now by Livy. It was, it wasn't, it *was* a pipe! She mustn't break it now, even if the Olmsteads had to go without her, even if she missed the train. Carefully, slowly, she brought the stone object out of its age-old hiding place, and jumped to her feet and ran for the drive, as she went rubbing the worst of the dirt off with her clean go-away handkerchief. She couldn't see that the pipe was broken. Not anywhere.

Now the carriage had started up the hill, and Pamelia was running almost behind it, panting and rubbing the last of the dirt from the pipe as she ran. By this time she could make out something of the pipe bowl. It seemed to be a raccoon with a fish in its two little paws. Oh, it was beautiful and it *was* perfect!

Pamelia arrived in the dooryard of Indian Mound Farm almost as soon as the carriage did.

"Pamelia! You're a sight!" cried Aunt, but Pamelia scarcely heard her.

Pamelia was running through the vegetable garden gate, for once leaving it open behind her, while Pawnee Sam straightened to meet her, and in silence her earth-

stained fingers put the pipe into his earth-stained hands.

"It's a peace pipe, Sam," she said. "It is for my friend, just as in the old-time Indian days."

Sam looked at Pamelia. And now at last his eyes said a great deal to her. "My friend," he said slowly, and the words were his thanks.

"Pamelia!" called Aunt. "Come at once! Mr. Olmstead says he can allow you five minutes to wash up, and you may have my clean handkerchief."

So off Pamelia ran, with Livy lurching after her, leaving Pawnee Sam standing with the Mound Builders' pipe in his hand, staring after her.

"My goodness!" thought Aunt, catching a glimpse of his face, "Pawnee Sam is actually smiling!"

Livy's Song

How peculiar human beings are—even Pamelia!
Though I admit she's the nicest human
    being that I know.
They're so often in a hurry, they don't know
    what's important.
They'll give even a grasshopper only a glance
And then, off they go!

Pamelia is better than the others. She'll
    sit thinking.
She carries cookies in her pocket,
    and always gives me my share.
Her grasshoppers must be in the clouds or
    off beyond the horizon.
She looks and looks and looks.
I must quack to say that I'm there.

Pamelia is prettier than people, and
    kinder than other geese are,
She lets me go everywhere with her. Perhaps she
    is lonely, too.
She's good to me and somehow or other—how can
    a goose tell? —
In the end I did something to make her happy,
I, poor lame Livy, I found the right thing to do!

ELIZABETH COATSWORTH first made her mark as a poet; and poetry, by her own statement, remains her real calling. Her first volume of poems, *Fox Footprints,* was published in 1923.

The author of more than sixty books for young readers, Miss Coatsworth is considered one of the truly distinguished writers for children of this century. In 1931 she won the Newbery Award for *The Cat Who Went to Heaven,* and in 1968 she was honored as first runner-up for the Hans Christian Andersen Award, the only international award given an author for his complete work.